MAX'S BOOK

MAX'S BOOK

MAX'S BOOK

Other
Poems

Richard Rollins

Seaplane Press

Max's Book
Copyright © 2023 by Richard Rollins

Printed in the United States of America

Cover Illustration by Tom Thompson

Seaplane Press
Portland, OR

LCCN: 2023915147
ISBN: 978-1-7371412-4-2

Other Poems

No. 1

"Something about October, something..."
Love is in it
Your son is there
"What was it happened in October?"

She rolled the wheelchair back
Outside, it was snowing
"Pills," said the nurse
Her hands trembled to the cup

"Something wrong...did I do something wrong?"

No. 2

Wind
It was late Saturday afternoon
Cold

"Jesus,
    the light's gone out again-
    David?"

"Oh no,
    that's not going to be good enough,
    see?"

Heavy snow
    drifted against the rear of the house
Five o'clock

"Please...
    I just want to go home"

No. 3

"Well, it wasn't supposed to be that way"
"Baby?"
"What?"

Falling snow
Fire popping
Up on the roof the cat curled against the chimney

"Don't"
"I wasn't going to do anything...honest"
"Just don't"

No. 4

"Odd that you should think..."
"We were just wondering about you,
    that's all"

Dust
Men shouldering against one another
Grass beat down from heavy feet

"Why don't you just come with us?"

No. 5

"What'cha looking at over here, boy?"
Scraps
Paper
Lines settled flat

Hurt
"That's the price you have to pay"
Pain

"Not what I expected"
"Never is is it"
"Hope?"
"Hope is all we have"

"And fear"

No. 6

What if what you say is not true?
What if what you say is not accurate?

"Didn't I?"
"What?"

"Love you"
"No"

"This hand I place on this heart"
"Puh-leeze"

No. 7

"Did you know…"
"Would you?"
Seventeen days before it all came unglued
Rock
Bent steel

There's a lazy drift to it right now
Dozens of boys down by the water
Cold
A bitter wind blowing across the plains
      piling up drifts twenty feet high

"Clara?"

No. 8

"What was all the ruckus about?"
Dead
Flat

Grass grew down through the gully
Water, glass, bits of broken metal
"Well?'

Food
"There's a bit of a pretty thing"
"Not now"

"Gone"
Wind, snow, the smell of black pine

No. 9

"Who the hell do you think you are?'
"Not now...
     please..."
"Now"

Rain
Ground slick with mud

"Do wounds ever really heal?"
"Never"

Blood
Fool
White
"All pray"

No. 10

"For pity's sake"
"I can't"
"There's no harm in trying...there's no
    harm in that"

Grass moved at the edge of the water. Sunlight
    fell on cold rock
Dawn

Drowned again
Over and over...weight, water, body gone limp

"Does anybody here know what time it is?"

No. 11

Breath
Cold
Seven

It was late, all the lights were out
"Will you?"
"I...I can't"
"Pleeeze"

Then she turned,
    her hair wild

"Not now"
"Not ever"

Evening of the first day

No. 12

"Saludo"
Horses
Sweat

Nine times out of ten
"So you say"

All around the country was barren,
    overgrown with thistle and stump weed

Christ in his mercy
"So you say"
"What?"

No. 13

"Wait"
"Don't shine those shoes"
"You said"

 In the end all the seeds blew away
"David?"
"Not here you don't"

"Oh, for the love of Christ"
 Water
 Drift
 Land blown back against itself

"All rise"

"What was it?"
"Ah"
"And so..."

We were all late
We were all behind the times
"But still..."

Rock & tree
Sand & water

"Haven't we eaten enough?"

No. 15

"No juice flowing"
"Scratch it up"
"Scratch it up"

Outside the window, trees heavy with snow
"Oh, David, could you please?"
Birds hopping up on the split rail fence

"What do we know?"
What do we really know?

Aces
Frogs
Cattle... breaths steaming onto the cold

"Now this,
    is what I call
    fine dinning"

No. 16

"Huh...sure"
"Only now, now"
"Ah"

Wind over the hills
Smell of bacon frying
"Tonight"

"It wasn't fair,
    it just wasn't"

Wine
Women
Song of my father

"Let me bleed,
    okay?"
Let me bleed

Craw
Vapor
Ride a dark horse

"It wasn't me,
    it wasn't"

Small broken twigs
The nature of the stars
"Even if we could,
    it wouldn't be right"

Wave upon wave
Apples, pears, persimmons
The right to die

"Don't think for a minute,
    I take this lightly"

No. 18

"Wha'cha looking at?"
"Never seen hair on a dog's ear before"
 Beauty
 The right shade of green

"It won't be but a minute now"
"Damn...and damn again"

 Spain in early April
 The ground dry, crumbles underfoot
 Sea breeze
 Cry of a great white bird

"I've been thinking"
"Please pass the plate"
"Baby...I've been..."

"Rats"

No. 19

"What's in a name?"
Braver
Denser
The rate of return

Walk out over these hills
Snow falling
Twigs
Wet leaves

"Do we believe?"
"Yes"
"Do we know?"
"No"

Wasted
The hand moves across the eye
Defeated
The mouth shapes a slow grin

"Would you now?"
"Yep"

"Didn't we?"
"Didn't we what?"
"If you had asked,
     I would have"

 Wheat
 Dry grass
  Sound of moaning
"What of it?"

"I didn't know,
     I didn't"

"Would you have?"
 Tires
 Springs
 The slow arc of her arm

"Hold that door!"

Burn the roses
"We'd all hunkered down and then,
    Avery here..."
"Do you suppose we could just let it go?"
"Maybe"

The patter of little feet
 China in the closet
"Warm are we?"
"Not on your life"

"Oh, no"
 Slippery when wet
 Deadfall
 The high cost of living
"Crumbs, is it?"

"That's the most preposterous thing I ever heard"
 Knock
 Rattle
"Lie still"

"Do this"
Peaches
Rabbit
"All about what?"

"Well, it finally came out, but it wasn't
    as if we didn't have to pull like hell"
"Wake up...this ain't going to be pretty"

Died
Two by two
"All cease"

"Mother?"

No. 23

Weight of snow
Bend of elbow
"Do you really?"
She said...He said

It wasn't long after that that all the
    birds began to die
"We saw them coming from the East,
    big balls of greenish light"

A good day
Wicker
Hungry
"Don't you see?"

"A chance to believe again"
"Not bloody likely"

Cut
Rake
"Slice the pie, Alice"

"Wha'cha doing?"
"Didn't you say...?"
Weep
Hour after hour

"We took the whole country"
"Not a day goes by I don't think of him,
    not one day"
"Ain't that a hoot"

Wells
Two day
Barrel of luck
"We gonna stay here, Jim?"

Apple
Butter
Sister, sister

"Please believe me"

"Well, it damn well was"
"That a fact?"
 Simple times
 Needle and thread

"Paul?"
 Eat
 Flavor
 Time of the month
"Is this for real?"

Between the house and the lake there were
     four pear trees set in a row
"I've been thinking. It's been over forty
     years since I heard a word"

"Don't tell the children"
"What if..."
"Just don't"

 Bird
 Hair
 A life of one's own

No. 26

"We were three seated on a beach"
 Smell of roasting meat
 Eucalyptus
 Butter

"Women come here to pray"
 Every day they kneel down by the rocks
"Lift their dresses"
 Wash themselves in the water

 January
 Late in the day
 The crowd began to turn ugly

"Come in, come in"
 Happily
"What a handsome man"
 Somber
 The catch of the day

No. 27

"Well?"
"Bite your tongue"
There were forty of them standing over
    by the barn
Caught

Highway
Touch
"Ask the price"

November
The ache of the unknown
"Wouldn't it have been better if you'd
    let out a little more line there?"
Saving grace
"All right?"

Whipped
"Get up off your knees and don't you never
    let me see you kiss the floor again"
"Think I hear mother calling"
Sold

No. 28

Awake
The arm at rest
Pity

"We were born into this world
    without expectation"
"Humor me"
Lost
Eve of destruction

"Will this be suitable?"
"Time's run out"
"I'm not sure there's any need
    to be quite so formal"
Blink
"Touch me"

Said
Return
"Help is on the way"

No. 29

"Most of this we can appreciate"
"Although it's not inevitable"
"There was a time when I felt very sick,
    very ill at ease"
"Do you dance?"

Rain
The wind blew, tossing the tops of trees
"Don't wait for me"
The river turned and made a bend
    against the high wall of rock
Everywhere one looked there were the bones
    of small animals

Summer
"Stunning"
Away for the weekend
"Help yourself"
"A real bloodsucker, that one"

"It ain't what you say that counts"
"There's a bigger dog here now"
"Honey?"
"Would you turn out the light"

Light came in through the open window
"The sooner the better"
At the end of the street, mine tailing spilled
     across acres of dead grass
"You can take my word for it"

Happy is he that is first
"Wake me when it's over"
The garage door slammed shut
"And I suppose I'm supposed to understand that?"

Heavy shoes
Race against water
"We bought it on sale"

Eggs, butter, cream
The sign of the times
"Pick it up, asshole!"

"We'd of been killed"
"Easy to say"
 White
 Fire popping in the fireplace
"It'll just take me a minute to spruce up"

 Old man
 Sitting
 Day gone by
"Pa?"
"Damn, that son-a-bitch climbed right up my
     pant leg"

 Easy on
 Weight on the left foot
 Neither hide nor seek
"When's that sucker gon' be cooked?"

"Let us in"
 Let us in

No. 32

"Wouldn't that have been fine"
 Gooseberries
 Pumpkins
"The rest of the lot"

"How about we all just swing"
"Too late"
 Pond
 Ice
 Ringing in the ears

"Could we stay up all night...could we, huh?"
 Radio plays
 Sheep
 Nick from a knife
"All right"

"It wasn't always this way"
 Stunts
 Rattle in the throat
 Big

"Help me, now"

"Do not touch!"
White washed
The angry sea
"I'll jump on that"

"Wouldn't it be revealing..."
"If you say so"
Chums
"In a heart beat"

"We could have lost everything"
"Didn't I say..."
Remorse
Twist of envy
"Play your cards right"

Shatter
Dance
"Fuck off"

"Would you now?"
Easy on
Try

"What ever happened to all the beautiful people?"
The sky was clear and filled with wild birds
"Seven of us couldn't hold him"
Wind swept up the valley,
    creating a deadly blast

"Save your knickers"
Wood
Pistol
The sign of an early grave

"Darcy?"
"If everyone would just kiss someone on the ear,
    the world would be a better place"
"Okay"
"Time to shuck the corn"

"Was that the sound of a door closing?"

"Who do you think you are?"
Candy
Rest
The whole nine yards

"Alright break it up"
Flag
Purchase
"You can't get any fucking sleep in here"

In the early evening a warm breeze came
     down from the hills carrying with it
     the smell of pine
"Whadaya say?"
"Broke...I'm broke...no...money"

Rust
Light
A baker's dozen
That was the night he finally settled down
     in the big chair by the fire and poured
     himself a bourbon and water

"Smells like the cat died"

"Holy cow"
 Roses of sunset
 Beach balls
 Snap of elastic garters

"I wish it was over"
 Too soon
 Two weep
"Heaven help the deaf"

"We were born in a box in the back
    of my Uncle's barn"
"The Forth of July was the best present
    I ever got"

"Ladies and gentlemen"
 Whistles
 Toots
 The sound of an old guitar

"Put your dancing shoes on, Darling"

"Eclipse the moon"
"Wary of the ol' eye are yuh?"
 Sack of grain
 Auto

"We reap the chattel"
"Spoken like a true vamp"
"Where's the pleasure?"
"Oh, Baby, touch not"

 Eat and die
 Flour and sugar
"He who bites first, bites last"
"Correct me if I'm wrong"

"Not a sound, now"
"Okay, what?"
"Whimper to heaven"
"There's no need to be tactless"

 Angel
 Dust
 Broken toys of disillusionment
"Ralph, shut it down...we're a little
    backed up here"

No. 38

"Whoa"
"That buck won't bite"
"Save it for me"
 Dilapidated
 Left out in the rain
"Would you care for another turn at the organ?"

 It had been some months since the last
     train had passed through town
 Chickweed
 Dance
 The sigh of regret

"Who opened this door?"
 Beggars
 Draftsmen
 People of ill repute
"Wouldn't it be fine if we all had ten dollars
     to spend any way we wanted"

 Daughter
 Ache
 Pistol of love
"Keep you damn hands to yourself"

No. 39

"Can't get enough"
 Diamonds and jewels
 Turning right
"This way, this way"

"Would you be my friend?"
 Apples of distrust
 Speed of contentment
"All aboard"

A great swath of grass spread
    down to the river
The fire burned into the evening,
    brick and mortar falling
    smoldering to the sidewalk
"Ain't she the cutest little thing?"

 Dope
 Pebbles
 People of substance
 Arguably

"John...let the cat out"

"Sooner than that"
 Lack of remorse
"Bend down, bend down"

"What luck"
 Shake the rattle
"Help boys"
 Whisper of kindness

"Will you help me undue this dress?"
 Brokenhearted
 Memories of dust
"In some places wounds never heal"

"Kiss me"
 Starlight
 The back of a hand
 Moonlight
 The blue of the lake
"Kiss me"

"Not so fast there, Jim"

No. 41

Dead weight
The sound of stone
"Wake me"
"Let the children go out and play"

"Who could have guessed"
Right hand
Left hand
"All fly away"

"Dorothy, come into the bedroom I want
    to show you something"
"It's remarkable how men squirm
    about in their chairs"

Often
The last hope
"That's my best offer"
Tea
Meadow
The cusp of the moon

"Fire it up, Honey"

No. 42

"Moved, I am"
 Broken
 Twisted
 The heart rendered

"Wake up"
 Bounce
"Eat your fill"
 Ogle

"The eyes, the eyes"
 Weep
"Best foot forward"
"How absurd"

It was late. All the lights were out. He heard
    a faint creaking as of someone opening a door
There were two of them. One leaned against the barn
    with a rifle resting in his arms

Fish
 The naked truth
"Down we go"
"Pull in, pull in"

No. 43

"Eight, wasn't it?"
"The time you said…"
"Don't shake it"
"Never"
 Anger at the smallest interruption
"Could we please have our tea now?"

"Do they bite?"
 Aspirin
 Asparagus
 The price of a new car

"We came all the way from Cincinnati"
"There was a grapefruit stopping up the toilet"
 Gun shy
 Wiseacre
"Better to be inquisitive"

The road forked and went down into a dry wash
    with sage and rabbit brush and a golden eagle
    casually perched on a mesquite branch

No. 44

Blue
River
The niceties of life
"It wasn't that"

"Don't break that"
Before dawn
Appalled
The right to die
"Wake me when it's over"

Tired
Bereft
The call of the tide
"Haven't we eaten here before?"

"Now, for the last laugh"
"Broke your heart, did he?"
"Buggers"
"Ow!"

"Suddenly, the shade snapped up and
        I almost jumped clean out of my skin"

"Details, details"

"Whatever happened...?"
"Okay, that's it"
 Maple
 Bird
 The twist of delight

"We can't see"
"Do not..."
 Whisper
 Dew
"Ah, the last straw"

"Weep, yuh"
"All together now"
 Play
 Day to day
"We receive this with humble approval"

 Cats
 Sad
 Echo of remorse
"Don't rock"

"Nah"

No. 46

Witchy
"Way to go, Bud"

"Divorce?"
"Why not?"

The right light
    dances over us all

"Be at peace"
"Easy enough
    for you to say"

Too bad
"You bet your
        blue ass"

Too want
"Hold that pose"

In the name of...
"I believe"
" I make to come out of..."

"Saw this sucker"
Make it sing
Cast off
"Cast off"

No. 48

Consume
The stars of night
    eat their own lack of space
Beware

"And this helps...how?"
"All that it seems
    to be...it is"

Would...you?
Could...you?

"Stand still"
"Don't make me get up and go to
    the window one more time"

"Aux armes"
 Aux armes
 No great shakes
"Dance, Little Tiny, dance"

No. 49

"And, Willard?"
"You make me sick"
 Dash of pepper
 Pinch of spice

"Wake up, Baby, wake up"
 Long train coming
 Whipsaw
 Lack thereof

"It would have been nice if I could
     have counted on you just once"
 Amble
 Slip
"Who would have thought it to look
     at me that I had spiritual aspirations"

 A dozen thoughts
 A simple twist of mind
"Could you help me?"
"Would I?"

 Fingers together
 Lips apart
"Ah, yes"

No. 50

This eats this heart
"You made a
     muck of it"
"What's that?"

 Cry
"Okay, I've got the reach"
"Take the number two bus
     and get off by the laundromat
"Coffee?"

"You think you're so smart"
"You think you own me"
 Blind as a pig
 Weighed down every day
"Tired?"

"Caught you off guard,
    didn't I, Baby?"
 Sex
 Surrender

"Love, ya!"

No. 51

"They stare and stare"
 Wives
 Husbands
"I wondered about that"

 The empty bed
 The broken heart
"Gees, Honey, I..."
"Eat dirt!"

 Why
...so in the evening when the children
    had been put to bed,
    they sat by the fire reading
    and sometimes holding hands"
"John?"
"It's gone. It's not my fault. It's
    not"

 Signs of lowered prices
 Dust gathered on the sill
 Pools of oil

"Wha'cha got there, Squirt?"

Four square
Righteous indication
Two heathen attempts
"So you say"

"What calls you?"
Dewdrops
The response of a smooth hand
"I'd eat all that, Ma...but there's
        no 'tatters"

Thistle
Chickweed
Angle of shadow
"Save me?...sure...
        you could have"

"Once I was pretty too"
The blink of an eye
No one called
"Oh, Daddy, why?"

No. 53

"I ain't saying and you can't
        make me"
 Back door open
"Here's your change"
"What?"

They were waiting at the end of
        the block. One of the men was
        leaning against the car, his hand
        in his pocket
"Picture of Christ is forty cents"
 Make it two
"Dogs remain seated"

Under the window, two small thorn
        bushes grew red berries
"I ate already"
 This happy month
"Would you please step over this way
        and put your hands flat
        against the wall"

"Now you think"
"Now, you say you're sorry"
"Oh, look at the lateness of the hour"
"Wet?"
"I'd give my right eye for a piece of ass
        like that"

"Don't"

Fester
The life blood of whippets
Too reason, too soon
"And so they were married…"
"Don't cha' know"

"Once, when I was a little boy, I
    saw a man all limp and hanging
    in a barn"
"Trouble the children to come unto me"
"If it were between a poke and a fiddle,
    I'd take the fiddle every time"

The door swung open
"Say…who's gone?"
"Taylor?"
The rest of us hid down in the swamp

Confusion
"I might say the same"
Back of the hand
"Don't you never say that again"

"Is it getting warm in here,
    or is it just me?"

No. 55

Cough it up
The right of refusal
"Add to that"
"Whoa"

"To be blunt, that sucker'd look better
    dead"
They came out of the store with their arms
    loaded down with packages
"I can't cry anymore"

Nestled together, soft and with their
    naked bodies entwined
"Shhh..."
"Now I lay me..."
So and so and so

This then is the beginning
"Time and tide, ect., ect."
"Wouldn't you love to stand in the
    snow with the wind screaming
    all around you?"
"Well, now, ain't you the pretty boy?"

"Guess"

Dis this
Throw in the towel
"Better to be a beggar"
"Shut yr yap!"

He got up slowly and went to the window.
    It was snowing. Large flakes drifted down
    through the branches of the pines.
"Well, what are you going to do?"
"Mary, Mary, Mary"
Simple

Get off the bed
Waste not
Want not
"Better to be born face down"

"Didn't you know he'd say that"

No. 57

Pool
The fingers rippling
"Wise men once said all that we are
     we become"
"Hope not"

"To die is to be reborn"
"What a load"
"Don't knock it if you haven't tried it"

Curse
Spittle
She wandered along the shore
"Seems to me it'll be all right"

"What day is this?"
End of the world
Right to die
"Oh, bother"

"Well said"
"Hear, hear"
"Forget it!"
"Shhh...listen"

"I..."

No. 58

"Quick!"
"Cut that throat"
"Monster"
"Say, pal"
"Evil is not the absence of anything"

The moon rose late. Snowflakes fell
    into the river and the banks were
    deep in snow. Otters slid and
    splashed and shook water from their
    dark coats.
"All right you want to get out. Then
    get out and stay out. I never
    want to see you again. I hate you!
    I hate you!"
The bear moved slowly up the side
    of the hill stripping berries with
    its tongue. From time to time, it
    stopped to turn over rocks and lick
    up ants and beetles and look for
    ground squirrels.

 Leaves
"What of the wind?"
"If I could wish for one thing,
    I would wish for more courage"
"You don't say?"
"Easy, now"

"Hon?"

No. 59

"To sleep perchance..."
"It's the little things..."
The wooden fish
The clock
Daylight

They built the fire on the wet sand
     at the end of the gravel bar
She bought another round of
     shooters and beers
"There were plenty of potato chips
      this morning"
"Oh, God, it hurts so bad!"
She eased the lever forward and then let out
     her breath

Pieces of glass
Empty chairs
"I never wanted to hurt you. I never
      did"
Refrigerator left open
Dishes in the sink
"All quiet?"

"I've been there and I can tell you
      it's not much"
"Give us a hand here will ya? This
      sucker weighs a ton"

No. 60

"Weep ya"
"Two ducks for a dollar"
 There was a big man sitting at one
        of the tables in the back
        with a plate full of spaghetti
        in front of him
"I wouldn't know"

"How now little brown cow"
 Con
"That ain't right"
 Bitch
"Be right there, Honey"

"Do we really know so little?"
 Affirmative
 In the evening the deer came out
        of the trees and moved slowly
        toward the salt lick, their ears
        forward, their eyes wide
"Didn't you never sleep up in the hay
        with the loft doors kicked wide
        and the snow drifting in?"

"It's my last one. Here...you have it"
 Buttercups
 The side of an old barn
"Pleased to meet cha!"

No. 61

"Can't be me"
"I would have come"
"Don't know, I don't"
"Twern't natural"

The wind moved the grass, laid it almost
    flat and turned the undersides of the leaves
    up silvery in the moonlight
"I've always lived a simple sort of life"
It was down deep. They dug all through the night
    and by morning they still hadn't found it
"Wha'cha looking at?"

Desire
The slip of a dress
"Who goes there?"
"Shhh...Hon...it's alright"

"I don't want to die, I don't"
This side up
Open from the top
"Could we have a little more light
    over here?"

No. 62

Happy chuckling laughter
"From the corners of your eyes"
Soap, tomatoes, glycerin
"We are beloved of God"

Down the long dusty road, past
    rotting bales of hay and abandoned
    farm equipment...
"Nobody knows, huh? Nobody knows?"
Cocaine from Las Vegas
Snow in the mountains
Untimely deaths

"I will be absolutely frank with you"
Naked
Stretching under cool sheets
"Here, you hold the baby"

"On the other hand, their will always be evil"
"And why not?"
Curse the luck
"But...Baby?"
"Wake up!"

No. 63

Polishing stone
Butter in the hand
The mind regards itself
"Pick up that mess"

Water running
The brown turn of an otter
Speckled eggs among the down
"Say yr piece an' get out"

Winsome
Smell of warm breath
Taste of another tongue
"That's right pal, end of the line"

"Don't we want to do what's right?"
"Who's to know"
"Check the time, Dave"
"Nothing's true that can't be shot"
"Oh, that's bright"

Winter is a happy time
"I've saved and saved and saved"
Storms blow in from the the West and are gone
"Quit...that's it...I quit"
"Best of luck to ya"

No. 64

Too near the stars
The distance of...
"I don't really know why I love you"
"I don't know if I do"

"We were all together holding hands"
"Dad?"
How is immortality to be befriended?
What is the right way to brush your teeth?

"Seven days ago I weighed over one hundred pounds"
The lights came on and they saw
    the living room in shambles
"I can still remember when it was
    easy to think the right thing"

"You don't know fear until you've been
    afraid of your own thoughts"
Wouldn't of...
Couldn't of...
Shouldn't of...
"I never show respect to anyone
    unless they earn it"
"Save me some of that, will ya?"
"Oh, Honey"
"Next up!"

No. 65

He wasn't who he thought he was
"Makes sense"
"What?"
"All aboard!"
It was past midnight when the car pulled
    up and stopped in front of the Italian restaurant
    on the corner opposite the church

"Darling?"
"You don't know how much I miss touching you"
Then the theater lights went out
"Hey, don't shove"
Constant fear of the unknown

In the morning he pushed up the window
    and heard pigeons cooing on the ledge
"Eight o'clock, time to get up"
Smell of toast
Smell of delight
"Come on back here to bed, why don'cha"

Soft, soft, soft
"Why do you weep so?"
"Sometimes I think I'll go mad if I can't
    eat everything and everyone"
"Okay, okay...put away the knife"
Doors unlocked
"You said large...didn't you?"

No. 66

The slow temptation to submit
"Watch your step"
"Go on up to the corner and take a left
	in front of the bank"
Twenty days have November...

 We were all seated around the fire telling stories
"That's mine, you got your own"
"Help me hold this fucker down, will ya?"
 Snow blew in through the front door and
	drifted onto the rug

"You done a good job, boy"
 There was no place to go, the trail
	had slid off into the canyon
"Don't take it literally"
 It was after seven when he stepped
	into the shower

"I'd love to see you naked"
"Wan'na bet?"
"Alright"
"Oh, my, god!"
"That's better"

No. 67

Englishman
"Sure you are"
Whipsawed little butt
"I've broken bread with the best
    of them"

"Nickel sized prick that is"
"Smarmy little toad"
"What you need is the back of a hand"

Any day now
Wishes
Sliver of light
The edge of a yawning maw
"That'n a good kick in the teeth"

The two men stood in the rain drinking, their
    coat collars turned up, their hats pulled
    down over their eyes
"Green Boys! Green Boys!...playing
    in the swamp!"
Arrested development
Commitment to God
Interspacial transfers
"It gets so a guy can't think around here"
"Put out the light"
"Oh...uh...sure"

No. 68

"What haven't I done?"
 Questions of remorse
 Questions of temerity
"The stars, the stars"

"Each and everyone of us needs to pick
    up his or her equipment and go
    to their assigned positions"
The man wept quietly at first and then
    his whole body began to shake
    with great sobs

Once upon a time...
The way it is
This one's for you
Meet me after work

"I don't care what you say, I can't
    smell a damn thing"
 Reason to worry?
 Gone for good?
"There's no help now"

"Oh, John, don't...please"

No. 69

He was doing business in another country
"You don't say"
Thoughts weighed heavily on his mind
"Were there animals...were there?"

"It's lovely to see you again"
"Size is of no consequence"
"The right shoe goes on the right foot"
"Hope for a better tomorrow"
"Why didn't I think of that?"

"Not bloody likely"
"Which way out of here?"
"Slight feeling of panic"
"Says who?"

"We were all blessed, but in the end
        it proved not to be enough"
The lights went out and people moved
        clumsily about the room
"They say that if you have enough
        faith you can move mountains"
The man bent over and picked up the bottle
        cap, rubbing it between his thumb
        and forefinger for a moment

"All rise"

No. 70

"It wouldn't be for me that you
        came all this way...would it?"
The man shuffled and spit
        into the dirt at his feet
"I say, Max?"
"Wipe your nose, Sonny"
The door opened and the little girl stepped
        out onto the sidewalk with the basket
        clutched tightly in her hands

"What do you know. It's eight o'clock"
Right to life
Mercy
Point of inspection
"Do you think it might be possible
        to open the window and get a little
        fucking fresh air in here"

Recumbent position
Tendency to decline
False representation
The need to know
"Maybe we could just nail a couple of two
        by fours over the door"
"You think?"

No. 71

Curl the feet
Curl the toes
"Oh, that is only illusion"
Here, between the shiny blades of wet
    grass, a small beetle has made its home

Raindrops on the tongue
Snowflakes on the lashes
"We've come to court you...every one"
"I thought it would be possible to
    sit idly by but I see now that
    that's not the case"

"We wish you well"
"Bienvenudos"
"The time that it takes to get from point
    A to point B is largely determined
    by attitude"
"If there are no other questions,
    you can put on your helmets"

Duty
The flick of a wrist
"Could I say something here?"
"Please do"

No. 72

"Who's responsible?"
 Down by the river the boat swung
    on its hawser on the incoming tide
"Excuse me?"
 The road went up over the hill and then
    turned and went past a large
    field of new mown hay
"Don't interrupt"
 She whispered and then turned her face
    toward him and he could feel her
    warm breath on his cheek
"Alright, alright, bring it here and I'll
    sign the damn thing"

 Bucket of blood
 The cat let out
"Who's to know?"

"Ladies and gentlemen, I appeal
    to your patience"
 The wind quit and he dug the snow
    out with his hands
 He wished he could remember what
    it was like to hold her
"It's too soon to cry, the worst
    is yet to come"

"We're going to be late, Dear"
"Oh, really?"
"Shhh"

No. 73

"...weighed in with his normal
        stupidity"
"There is no accounting for the dead"
"East of here, about four miles, there's
        an old tree folks calls the hanging tree"
The man got to his hands and knees
        and that was a far as he got

"For pity sake"
 Empty bags
"Ray?"
 Sun going down
"Kiss me...please"
 Cattle on the move

"Who's to say that a man doesn't hold
        his own life cradled in his hands"
"Now, there's a wicked thought"
"No turning back"
"Haven't we seen enough?"

 The loon
 The apple
 The smooth side of her face
"Pray for me"

No. 74

"You can't know the truth, why try?"
Turn of the hand
Small of the back
She came into the room and stood
    with the light falling onto her breasts

"We would hope that everyone here has
    brought his or her identity card"
Pissing in the alley
Twenty below and dropping
"If you had an once of courage, you'd
    stand up and tell everyone everything
    you know"

Hand on the door
Hand pushing back the drapes
Hand on the shoulder
"Have you ever met anyone you
    could trust...I mean really trust?"

She stood at the end of the bed, hands
    hanging by her side
"Here, kitty, kitty, kitty"
Outside the window, the moon
All over the world streetlights went off
    one after the other
"Yes...I will...will you?"

"Nailed that sucker to a tree"
"And then I said..."
Wind whistled through the leaves
Leaves scuttled along the ground

"Wha'cha do'n?"
"None of your damn business"
"We can't talk here"
"This is between you and me"

The car went up over a small rise
    and down a long hill
"We all believe in what we're doing"
He pulled the tire off and rolled it
    against the back wall of the garage
"One hand washes the other"

"Just suppose for a minute you really
    wanted to be honest"
The flight of geese came in low, honking
    and winging toward the gravel bar
"Let me make a call and see
    what I can do"
It was early and they were all seated
    around a large table.
"Please to meet you...and this is?"
"Damn your face"

No. 76

"Sit still"
The cows lumbered slowly along the barb
    wire fence through deep snow
"Where have all the robins gone?"
"On this day, many hundreds of years ago,
    some very important people came
    together and stood on this very spot"

"Don't cry for me"
Fracture
The call of a shrike
Fastidiousness
"Let's all be friends"

One woman could not be found
"Don't say it if you don't mean it"
They were bound to each other, not
    by family or history or even love,
    but by a sense of greed
"The past does not tell the truth about
    how it was, as the present does not
    tell the truth about how it is"

Whimper
The flight of an arrow
"Decode that"
"Okay"

No. 77

"Devoid of all reason"
The sun, the moon, the stars
"Here on earth we've come to believe
    in the finer things of life"
Conquer or be...

"This breath I give"
Hands held up
"Better crawl before you run"
Turn to look

"Who comes there?"
Naked in the dawn
Father, mother, daughter, son
"Don't just pick your favorite"

"Give me a chance, will ya?"
The lick of a lip
Hands on knees
"Don't kiss my ass"

"Well, I never..."
"Rude, isn't it?"
"Do you suppose it'd be appropriate
    if I cleaned up a little"
"Sit down, sit down"
"You'll be fine"

No. 78

81

Swaggering contempt
A likely story
"Everything always has extenuating
     circumstances"
"Do you like to fuck?"

Raw eggs
The hummm of a remote
"Pour me some more"
Rain on the windshield

"Smell that?"
In the beginning they huddled in
     front of the cave
The mailbox was empty but, then again,
     it had been for a long, long time
"Wish you were here"

"I've always wanted to be bright"
The sound of grass laying down
The flutter of an eyelid
"Would you come over here and lay
     your head in my lap?"

"Give me a minute"
"I love you...you know"
Alright now, all together
"Huh?"

Another conscious decision
"My, my, aren't we up early"
They came down the stairs arm and arm,
    smiling, laughing, happy to be leaving
"You don't waste much time, do you?"

"All that I need to know"
"Wouldn't that be nice"
There were alder leaves turning yellow
    in the crisp mountain air
He put the wrench down and wiped
    his hands on the oily rag

"Well, it's not much, but your welcome
    to it"
The film broke and suddenly the lights
    came on
"At that moment, your life is on hold"
"Oh, please"

Ten, nine, eight...
Wash your hands
"Did you ever find your keys?"
"I'd rather not talk about it"

Dime a dozen
Make or break
"Shut the door"
Running in the alley
"Hey, stop taking all the covers!"
"Little touchy, aren't we?"

No. 80

So her face...
"Seeing is believing"
Small of her back
"Look at me"

In the right place at the right time
"I always wanted to be fortunate"
Experience of a lifetime
"Believe me when I say: I...will...be...there"

No one home
Distant past
"Who's to know?"
"Don't bother knocking"

They picked up their bags and walked
    out of the bus station
Newspapers were stacked in the corner
He ran as hard as he could until he
    got to the corner and stopped
"Wait for me!"

Desperate
Without resolve
"Save yourself, Dave"
"D...d...des...ire"

Swirl of snowflakes
"Hell bent"
"Remember that last day?"
Roses climbing to the roof

"Let us pray"
"Oh, David, please don't"
"Join me for a drink, won't you?
"I didn't know what to do
     and I was afraid"

The man zipped up his jacket
     and pushed open the trailer door
"Fine, fine, if you say so"
The only sound was the ticking
     of snow falling through pine
"I wish I had a wife like that"

"There's plenty more where
     that came from"
He rubbed his hands together
     in front of the fire
"I couldn't help but notice"
"It's nothing"
Evening of the last day
"Can I get you anything...anything
     at all?"
"Please"

No. 82

"The message is clear"
 Chickens pecking in the dirt
"We could have been happy"
 Flattened tires stacked up in the sun

"My brother said..."
"Can it...dickhead"
 The wave of a hand
 A road down through the sand

"I was honest when I was a child"
 The people were seated in long rows
     and, when the curtain finally
     went up, they all cheered
"Don't be stupid...okay?"
 He raised his hand but the teacher
     never noticed
"Then there's tax"

"What was that?"
 Small change
 Minor inconvenience
"Let's make this brief then"

"It sure would be nice if all we had
     to do was sit here on the porch
     in the sun and drink beer and jerk off"
"Pshaw"

No. 83

"Ain't never, no sir"
"We was swimming and he jus' went down"
"Too bad you're late, son"
"Never mind"

The switch was high up on the wall, too
    high to reach
"Ain't but jus' the one of us here left now"
"Been down that road before"
 Sign said closed
"Bury it here"
"Me?"

"Like I told 'em, we was sitting over
    on the bench in the sun when it happened"
"It's kind'a like Arizona, if you don't
    look at the ocean"
"I once said I'd be back but it ain't
    gon'na be"
The four of them stood looking at the exact
    spot where the car had been
    less than ten minutes before

Weep
Pretty
"Bye, bye"
The last leg of a long, long trip

No. 84

Wetter and wetter
"Who'd have thought that"
Wit aside
"Purse those lips"

"Been here before"
"Natural for you"
"Ah, Baby"
"Welcome, welcome"

Do nothing
"Repeat after me"
Sa...ty..ri...a...sis"
"Gum shoe?"

They lost the last of all they had
"Will we be there by morning, Daddy?"
If she had time...but then...
"Wait for me...please!"

Some of us
Whisper
Many hearts
Believe
"I love in you"

No. 85

"You dreaming behind those eyes?"
And the light shifts
"Don't press it, Bud"
Women moving through the door
    into bright light

On the south side of the building,
    a beach stretched away to hills
    of dark green trees
"Let me sit here for a bit, would ya?"
The face that you love
The eyes of a friend

"When can we go home, Mommy?"
Wait
A moment too soon
Revere

Blind is as blind does
"What wouldn't I give to be able
    to do the right thing at
    the right time"
"Does this make any difference?"
"You bet your sweet ass it does"

Water
Smoke
The rest of the day
"I know, I know"

Too far in coming back...
"What'd you say?"
That's right, don't mess up
"Could we have a little quiet, please?"

"That was a long time ago"
"Put out your hand, Dear"
"Bet'cha...I don't"
"Now, John"

"When we were little, I always
    said that it wouldn't be fun
    growing up and I was right"
There were four cars in the front
    yard with the wheels gone
    and the doors ripped off
"If you never tell me the truth again,
    it'll be too soon for me"
"An' we was all they had left, me
    an' Buddy and Molly"

Wire
Door held open
"Diddy Dawg?"
"Samantha, you get your sweet
    ass over here"
Such an such an such

No. 87

Reached out
"No plan?"
Into emptiness
"Not what you thought?"

"What's that sound?"
"So then she said to me...she said,
    Max, don't...but I'd already
    turned away"
Courage
"There's plenty of folks wants to be brave
    and talks like they be brave, but the
    thing itself is something most folks
    don't actually know nothing of"

Wait
Ripe
Bittersweet
Heavy with remorse

"Can we go now, Aunt Polly?"
Hush
Rain on the ground
"Please believe me, I do like to dance"

No. 88

"Wipe yr nose yr little snot"
"In the morning, in the morning"
Rain pouring down
It's all about sleep

"Wish we could"
Dream
The back...the broken horse
"Have pity"

Too much
"That's the last of what I had"
So?
"You could have waited for me"

Despite
There were a growing number
    of people and they all
    desired the same thing
The car turned the corner
    and was gone
She closed the door
    and went back up the stairs

No thoughts
Wreck of a broken marriage
"What hospital did you say?"
"Turn off that light!"

No. 89

Deviousness
The right to lie
"Just once I'd like to know the
        meaning of my life"
"Pick a number and get in line"

It was mid-winter and he was happy
        in the soft crunch of snow
        and the dry grass bent down
"I've been meaning to tell you that
        I really appreciate that you think
        about the things you do
        and then talk about them"
She couldn't decide and then, because
        she was afraid, she decided to ask
"I've always thought that everything should
        go the way I expected it to go"

A rapid rise in temperature
"Wait for me"
Bus gone again
"Can you take me home now?"
"It's the least I can do"

"Say it's not true"
"Sorry?"
Monday again and again
Last days of a long difficult life

No. 90

Distance reclaims simplicity
The flight of an angle
The ease of remorse
"Don't butter that bread"

"I've always wanted to see
    what's really there"
Nine by twelve are the dimensions
    of reality
"Could you step a little closer
    and into the light"
Unwanted, uncared for, unloved

Then there was the sound of...
The sky was filled with stars that...
"Would you please sit down
    beside me"
"Suit up...suit up"

Devotion
One by two
Each his own
Time to go

"I've waited a long time for this"
"Could I be of any help?"
"Say what?"
"Oh, please"

No. 91

 Chickens in the yard
"Yellow?"
 Right of refusal
"You don't say"

"We floated out on the tide, gulls crying,
    wind blowing in from the sea"
"Seventeen miles would be my
    best guess"
The danger was obvious but not without
    a certain sense of satisfaction
Several people stood looking down at
    the dead birds at their feet

"Why would I believe that?"
 Obvious imperfections
 The right to untruth
"And you told me I could trust you"

 Stand or kneel
"Oh, Baby, let me hold you"
"What kind of life is this"
"And the expectation?"

"Give it to me"
"Sorry"
 Obvious laughter
 Obvious surprise

No. 92

"Would that I could"
"Broken now"
"Ah, I've so much to learn"
"Here, let me help you"
 Heal

They were walking down a long road,
    scuffling the dust at their feet
"There's plenty of room"
The man looked up at the stars,
    at the Great Bear
"It would have been difficult, it's true,
    but I would have done it for you"

"Can't we be friends?"
 Over and under
"Why waste time"
 Picture of his mother

"Soup's on"
"What?"
"Don't lie to me"
"Shhh"
"Be still"
"Oh, I do so wish..."
"Come in...please... come in"

No. 93

Weep
 Mary our Mother
"Hear me"
"Open your arms"

 Tsk-tsk
 Appeal
 The right to divine love
"Bring plenty if you come"

"Do you think it would be possible
     to wipe your feet?"
 They were not alone and they knew
     it was not a failure of strength
     that would be their undoing
"Save it for the loved ones"
 Then the wind shifted and the snow
     began to drift high up against
     the back of the shed

"People...please be seated"
 What is defined
 An unholy thought
"Beware the ice"
"Really, Doris!"
"Consider this then"
"Not blooming likely"

No. 94

"Do you think so?
 Wait and be rewarded
 Better buy now
"Says you"

 Deliver
 Rejoin
 Express yourself
"Pump it up"

"We lay down together and she put her hand
      on my back and I really was at peace"
"Don't be mistaking my good intentions
      for desire"
"Who would have suspected that the road
      would turn back on itself and go North"
"Eighteen years. I waited eighteen years
      and weren't none of it worth it"

"Say goodbye, Mary"
 Help is on it's way
 When she spoke, they all looked
"Nice day for it, don'cha think?"
 All the time
 Rest your bones
"Height?"
 We will be pleased
"Not now"

No. 95

"Hey, see your way?"
"I am coming"
"Wan'na talk?"
"Hear me crying"

 Round and round and round
"Don't want it, never did"
 Darkness and the stars
"Send it to me"

"I would like to go the way I was
     meant to go, be who I was
     meant to be"
 A strong smell blew down
     from the hill of rotting meat
     and dead fish
"What does it really mean to have courage?"
 Laying in bed in the dark, he began to sweat

 Palms open
"Come here"
 Door swung wide
"Take mine"

"In my left hand
     I hold my fate"
"Better buckle up"
"Kiss me first"

No. 96

Not one but two
"Beg'n yr pard'n"
 Right of entry
"Please remove your shoes"

"Could'a guessed"
"Sucker"
"What's right is right"
"What ever you do, for God's sake,
    don't bury me here!"

There was a small break in the fence
    and he pushed his way through
Somebody had broken the doll
    and left it out in the rain
The table wasn't clean, but then
    it was never clean, and no
    one knew why
"What I'd like to know is if there's
    ever been any sugar
    in this fucking house?"

 We compensate
"Pull up your pants, George, you're done"
 Flick of an eye
"I'll be seeing ya"
 Write

No. 97

Too weary
The weak link
"Alright, say it"
"Before you, me"

He was not very popular but it did
    not bother him and, in fact, he took
    comfort in the knowledge that ahead
    of him did not lay a lifetime of pretense
"If you stepped back out of the way,
    the rest of us could get through"
It wasn't always like this and he knew
    that if he kept his eyes open and his
    mouth shut he would see what it was
    he needed to see and be absolved
"Quit your damn moaning and be quiet...this
    won't take but a minute and it won't
    fucking hurt"

Soft as mud
Sacrifice
"Your barking up the wrong tree"
"What exactly then is wrong here?"
Guess

No. 98

Back fat
Drift
"Who comes here"
"Open wide"

"We take this into our mouths"
Push
"Not now"
Kneel
"No time like the present"

When all the people had left, he sat alone
    by the window waiting for the sunrise
"You're not crippled, you just think you are"
The boat rolled over slowly in the surf
    and went down
"These things are not supposed to matter"

"Do we really need this?"
"What you don't know..."
Second to second
Being born
"How fast was that?"
"Open your eyes"
"Piece of cake"

No. 99

Below the waist
"Talk to me"
"Saving it are you?"
"Wouldn't you like to know?"

Complete
The slow turn of a screw
"Your companions were brought in but I
     regret to inform you that they are
     all dead"
It was a great adventure but not
     the one he expected

Politeness carries great weight
"Be brave"
"It does not mean do not have fear"
In spite of all...

The bear clawed at his sleeping bag
     but he did not move
     and he did not cry out
"Every once in awhile I'd like to see
     the world as a beautiful place again,
     just to remind myself that it once was"

Desire to be reborn
Fear of failure
"Hold me"
"With pleasure"

No. 100

"Into the bright space of your heart"
"Tell me a story... please"
"Where it not for the rain..."
"So he came walking?"

The ordinary result of too much sugar
 Happiness as an antidote to life
"We have crackers...we need cheese"
"The point certainly escapes me"

 Expressing certain reservations
"Party time!"
 Inadequate communication
"Now that, was an orgasm!"

They held hands and slowly moved
     around the circle singing
He stopped suddenly when he saw
     the pig's head on the table
"Fourteen years ago I would a got
     a gun and shot that son-a-bitch"
"If you spill something, I expect
     you to wipe it up"

Daily remorse
Shuttling between beauties
Peace from afar
The rainmaker comes

www.ingramcontent.com/pod-product-compliance
Lightning Source LLC
Chambersburg PA
CBHW030904200726
48289CB00003B/889